DRAWING MANGA
VEHICLES

PowerKiDS press™

New York

Published in 2008 by The Rosen Publishing Group, Inc.
29 East 21st Street, New York, NY 10010

First Edition

American Editor: Victoria Hunter
Japanese Editorial: Ray Productions
Book Design: Erica Clendening
Coloring: Erica Clendening, Julio Gil, Thomas Somers, Greg Tucker

Manga: Masaki Nishida

Photo Credits: p. 23 (Fighter Plane, Bicycle, Helicopter, Monster Truck, Motorboat, Sports Car) © Shutterstock.com; p. 23 (Bullet Train) © www.istockphoto.com/ Karen Grieve; p. 23 © (Fire Engine) © www.istockphoto.com/Nick Schlax.

Library of Congress Cataloging-in-Publication Data

Nishida, Masaki, 1960-
  Drawing manga vehicles / Masaki Nishida.
    p. cm.   \ (How to draw manga)
  Includes index.
  ISBN-13: 978-1-4042-3848-0 (library binding)
  ISBN-10: 1-4042-3848-4 (libray binding)
 1. Motor vehicles in art \Juvenile literature. 2. Comic books, strips,
etc. \Japan \Technique. 3. Cartooning \Technique \Juvenile literature. I. Title.
  NC1764.8.M67N57 2007
  741.5'1 \dc22

                          2007012306

Manufactured in the United States of America

CONTENTS

The World of Manga

Manga is a **unique** Japanese form of art that borrows ideas from American **comic books**. It has always been very **popular** among Japanese people, and today manga is popular all over the world.

Manga **attracts** a wide **audience** because of its exciting stories that use a **combination** of pictures and **text**. The stories are easy and fun to read for any age **level**, from children to adults. All sorts of adventures can be created using manga. In this book we will draw eight vehicles in the manga **style** and will then show you eight stories based on those vehicles. After you learn to draw the vehicles, you can then create your own manga stories!

My name is Sayomi. Discover the **amazing** world of manga vehicles with Masaki and me!

Hi, my name is Masaki and I love reading and drawing manga! I know how to draw many different things in the manga style and have created all sorts of stories about history, sports, and adventure.

The supplies you will need to draw manga vehicles are:

- A **sketch** pad
- A pencil
- A pencil sharpener
- A ballpoint or a fine felt pen
- An eraser
- A ruler

Thank you for choosing to learn how to draw manga with us. We hope that this book will teach you how to draw manga vehicles and will **encourage** you to write and draw your own manga stories.

DRAWING A
FIGHTER PLANE

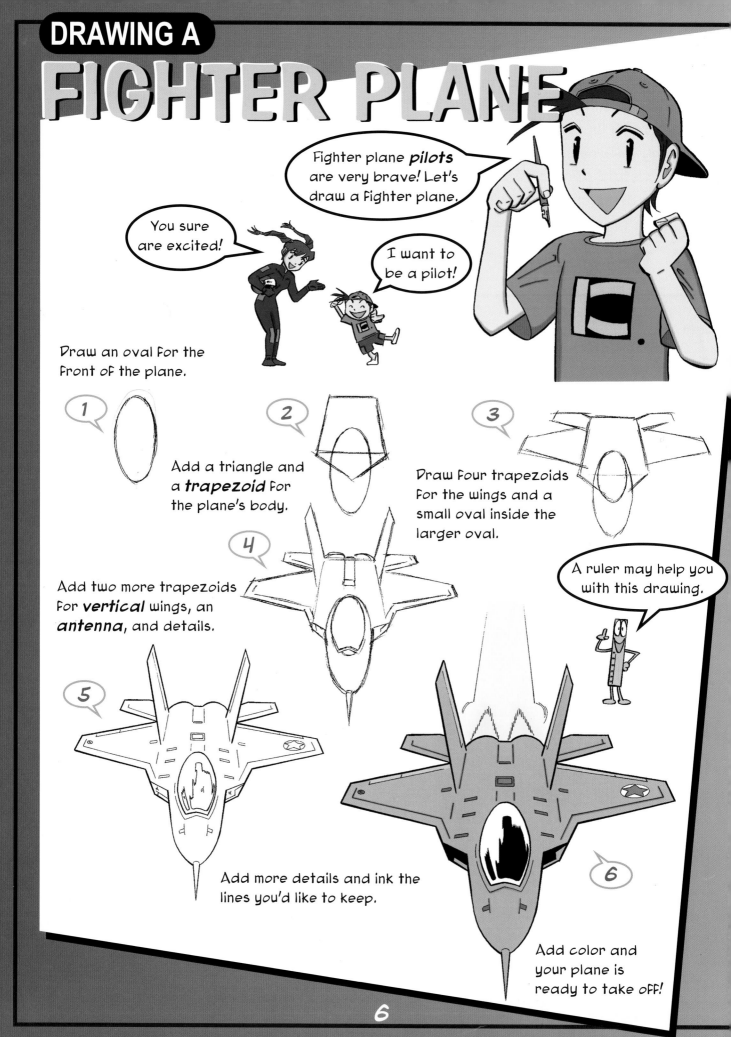

Fighter plane *pilots* are very brave! Let's draw a fighter plane.

You sure are excited!

I want to be a pilot!

Draw an oval for the front of the plane.

1

Add a triangle and a *trapezoid* for the plane's body.

2

3

Draw four trapezoids for the wings and a small oval inside the larger oval.

4

Add two more trapezoids for *vertical* wings, an *antenna*, and details.

A ruler may help you with this drawing.

5

Add more details and ink the lines you'd like to keep.

6

Add color and your plane is ready to take off!

THE CARROT ATTACK

DRAWING A
BICYCLE

I love bicycles. Let's draw a cool one!

Start with a pencil to sketch your bike.

1

Draw two circles, one slightly larger than the other, for the wheels.

2

Draw a small circle for the **gearbox**, and connect them all with the lines shown.

3

Add a triangle for the seat. Add the **handle** and backrest.

4

Draw the tires, frames, and **spokes**. Don't forget the chain! Now add ink.

5

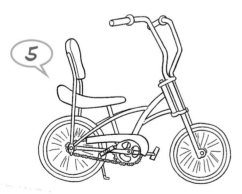

After using ink, erase the pencil lines.

6

Add color and shading, and your bike is ready to ride!

A SPECIAL BICYCLE

DRAWING A
BULLET TRAIN

High-speed trains are a really fast way to travel! Let's draw a Japanese bullet train.

1

Draw two circles and connect them with two lines.

2

Draw an oval at an angle, as shown, to create the front of the train.

3

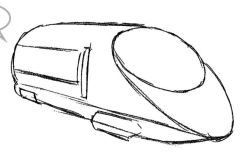

Add an oval for the *cockpit* and a rectangle for the window.

4

Add details such as the door, and then draw on the lines you'd like to keep with ink.

5

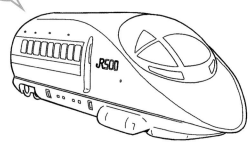

Erase pencil lines.

6

Add more details and color. Your bullet train is ready to zip away!

CATCHING THE BULLET TRAIN

DRAWING A
FIRE ENGINE

A Fire engine has the very important job of helping put out Fires. Let's draw one!

1 Draw a rectangle and square for the body.

2

Don't Forget the ladder!

Add three vertical lines. Then draw two circles and two half circles For the wheels.

3

Add windows, speakers, and the *bumper*. It's really starting to look like a Fire engine!

4

Add more details. Then draw over the lines with ink.

5

Erase extra lines.

6

Add color and shading to your Fire engine. Now it's ready to get to work!

THE COWBOY FIREMAN

DRAWING A
HELICOPTER

A helicopter can have many different uses. Here we're drawing a U.S. *military* helicopter.

1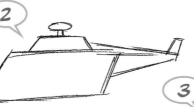

Draw a parallelogram for the body.

2

Draw a trapezoid for the engine, and add lines for the tail.

3

Add an oval for the upper *propeller*, and a circle for the rear propeller. Draw Xs in the center of each. Add windows.

4

Add more details.

5

After drawing with ink, erase the pencil lines.

Color in the helicopter and let's fly!

6

HELICOPTER TO THE RESCUE

DRAWING A
MONSTER TRUCK

It has huge tires and it can crush cars! Let's draw the supercool monster truck!

1

Draw a rectangular box for the body.

2

Add two more for the cockpit and *chassis*.

3

Draw thick circles for the huge tires.

4

Add more details.

5

Draw over the lines you want to keep with ink.

6

Erase the pencil lines.

7

Color in your truck. Crunch time!

THE GENTLE MONSTER TRUCK

DRAWING A
MOTORBOAT

There's nothing like a motorboat for speeding through the water. Let's draw one!

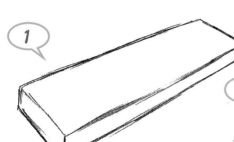

1 Draw a thin, rectangular box.

2 Divide the box into quarters and draw a triangle in the front.

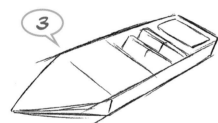

3 Add rectangles for seats and the engine room.

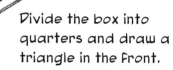

4 Add more details, such as a *windshield*.

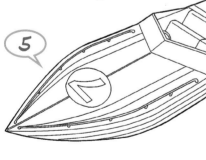

5 Draw on the lines you'd like to keep with ink. Erase the pencil lines.

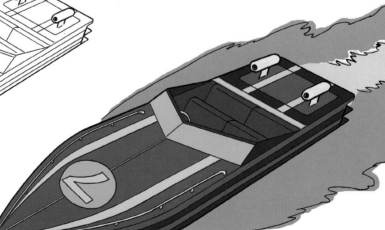

6 Color in your motorboat, and hop in! It's time to go for a ride!

THE MOTORBOAT AND THE SUN

DRAWING A
SPORTS CAR

For speed and style, a sports car is the car of most people's dreams!

1

Draw a rectangular box for the body.

2

Draw a triangle on top, and slope a line down to the back.

3

Add thick circles for the tires.

4

Round off the body, and add headlights.

5

Add mirrors and a bumper.

6

Add ink and erase the pencil lines.

7

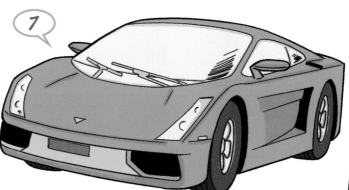

After coloring and shading, your sports car will be road ready!

THE NONSTOP SPORTS CAR

GLOSSARY

amazing (uh-MAYZ-ing) Filling with wonder.

antenna (an-TEH-nuh) A metal object used to send and receive signals.

attracts (uh-TRAKTS) Pulls toward.

audience (AH-dee-ints) A group of people who watch, listen to, or read something.

bumper (BUM-pur) A metal bar at the front and back of a car that prevents damage.

chassis (CHA-see) The part that holds up the body of a car.

cockpit (KOK-pit) The space in an airplane or other vehicle where the people who fly it sit.

combination (kahm-buh-NAY-shun) Something that is mixed or brought together.

comic books (KAH-mik BUKS) Books that tell a story using words and pictures.

encourage (in-KUR-ij) To give someone reason to do something.

handle (HAN-dul) A metal bar at the front of a bike that is used to brake and steer.

military (MIH-luh-ter-ee) Having to do with the part of the government, such as the army or navy, that protects its citizens.

pedal (PEH-dul) A tool that is pushed with a foot to make something work or move.

pilots (PY-luts) People who operate aircraft, spacecraft, or large boats.

popular (PAH-pyuh-lur) Liked by lots of people.

propeller (pruh-PEL-er) Paddlelike parts on an object that spin to move the object forward.

sketch (SKECH) A quick drawing.

spokes (SPOHKS) Rods that connect the middle of a wheel to the wheel's edge.

text (TEKST) The words in a piece of writing.

trapezoid (TRA-peh-zoyd) A four-sided shape with two parallel lines.

unique (yoo-NEEK) One of a kind.

vertical (VER-tih-kul) In an up-and-down direction.

windshield (WIND-sheeld) A sheet of glass that goes across the front of a car, truck, plane, or boat.

Meet the Vehicles!

Fighter planes
are used in the military for attacking other aircraft in the sky. They are small and fast.

Helicopters
are aircraft that can be used for military as well as recreational purposes.

Bicycles
are two-wheel, man-powered vehicles. They can be used for transportation as well as recreation.

Monster trucks
are modified pickup trucks with large wheels. They are used in shows in which they usually crush cars.

Bullet trains
are high-speed trains used in Japan. Called *Shinkansen* in Japanese, they can go about 300 miles per hour.

Motorboats
are small motorized boats. They travel on the water at high speeds and are primarily recreational.

Fire engines
are vehicles made to fight fires. They have hoses, ladders and other equipment firefighters need.

Sports cars
are performance-based vehicles. They are made to be beautiful, fast, and handle well.

INDEX